Sofia Takes the Lead

Based on the episode "The Buttercups,"
written by Doug Cooney

Adapted by Lisa Ann Marsoli

Illustrated by Character Building Studio
and the Disney Storybook Art Team

DISNEP PRESS

New York • Los Angeles

First Edition 10 9 8 7 6 5 4 3 2 1

ISBN 978-1-4231-8345-7

G658-7729-4-14024

Manufactured in the USA

For more Disney Press fun, visit www.disneybooks.com

Sofia is a Buttercup!
Mrs. Hanshaw is her troop leader.
Today Meg and Peg join the troop.

Sofia gives the girls their vests.
"You pin badges on them," she says.

"You get badges for doing things,"
Jade says.
"Like swimming or picking
flowers," says Ruby.

Sofia needs one more badge.
Then she will get a sunflower pin!

Tomorrow is her big chance.
The Buttercups are going on a
nature hike.

King Roland is worried.

He is afraid Sofia might get hurt.

"Baileywick will go along.
He will make sure you stay safe."

Sofia is ready to go.
So is Baileywick.

He was in a Groundhog troop.
"Groundhogs come prepared!" he says.

The hike begins!
Baileywick gives Sofia shade.

He clears her way.

He sweeps the path.

He keeps her cool.
Sofia wishes he would not help.

The girls stop to rest.
Baileywick pulls out a throne!
"I can sit on the ground," says Sofia.

The girls stop for water.
Sofia gets a fancy glass.

It is time to earn a badge.
The girls will build birdhouses.
Sofia gathers twigs to use.

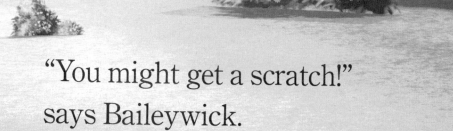

"You might get a scratch!"
says Baileywick.
He takes the twigs from Sofia.
"I can do it myself," says Sofia.

Mrs. Hanshaw looks at
Baileywick's birdhouse.
"Sofia, *you* were supposed to
build it," she says.

Ruby and Jade get badges.
Sofia does not.

Soon Sofia has another chance.
The girls can earn a badge for
getting wood.

Baileywick is worried Sofia
will get hurt.
He beats her to every log, branch,
and twig!

Baileywick holds up the wood.
"It only counts if Sofia does it,"
Mrs. Hanshaw says.

Everyone gets a badge but Sofia.
Jade even earns a sunflower pin.

The Buttercups stop for lunch.
Baileywick cooks for Sofia.

Sofia wants to do things for herself.
"Then I can earn my last badge.
And get my sunflower pin."

Baileywick promises to leave
Sofia alone.

There is one more chance.
The girls must pick daisies
and daffodils for a badge.

They must watch out for a bad
red plant.
It gives an itchy rash.

What if Sofia touches the
bad plant?
Bailey picks some red flowers
for her.

Baileywick's hands itch.
He needs the royal doctor.
But Baileywick cannot get down
the trail.

"We'll build a sled!" Sofia says.
She shows the Buttercups how.
The Buttercups are on their way!

Baileywick gets fixed up.
The king thanks him
for helping Sofia.

"She didn't need me at all,"
Baileywick says.
He tells how Sofia got him home.
"She's a leader, just like you."

Mrs. Hanshaw gives Sofia her badge.
Then Sofia gets a sunflower pin!
Baileywick gets something, too.
Now he is a Buttercup!